For Tom and Alice with love I.W.

For Alyx with love   R.A.

First published 1991 by
Walker Books Ltd, 87 Vauxhall Walk,
London SE11 5HJ

Text © 1991 Ian Whybrow
Illustrations © 1991 Russell Ayto

First printed 1991
Printed in Hong Kong by
South China Printing Co. (1988) Ltd

British Library Cataloguing in Publication Data
Whybrow, Ian
Quacky quack-quack.
I. Title   II. Ayto, Russell
823'.914[J]

ISBN 0-7445-2103-3

Quacky quack-quack!

Written by Ian Whybrow
Illustrated by Russell Ayto

WALKER BOOKS
LONDON

This little baby had some bread;

His mummy gave it to him for the ducks,

but he started eating it instead.

Lots of little ducky things
came swimming along,
Thinking it was feeding time,
but they were wrong!

The baby held on to the bag,
he wouldn't let go;
And the crowd of noisy ducky birds
started to grow.
They made a lot of ducky noises…

quacky quack-quack!

Then a whole load of geese swam up
and went **honk! honk!** at the back.

And when a band went marching by,
in gold and red and black,
Nobody could hear the tune –
all they could hear was…

honk! honk! quacky quack-quack!

"Louder, boys," said the bandmaster,
"give it a bit more puff."
So the band went **toot! toot!** ever so loud,
but it still wasn't enough.

Then all over the city, including the city zoo,
all the animals heard the noise
and started making noises too.
All the donkeys went...

ee-aw! ee-aw!

All the dogs went…

Woof! Woof!

All the snakes went…

SSSS-SSSSS!

All the crocodiles went...

snap! snap!

All the mice went...

squeaky ~ squeaky

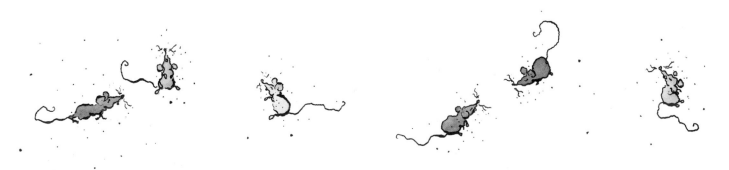

All the lions went…

roar!

Then one little boy piped up and said,
"I know what this is all about.
That's my baby brother with the
bag of bread;
I'll soon have this sorted out."

He ran over to where the baby
was holding his bag of bread
and not giving any to the birdies,
but eating it instead.

And he said, "What about some
for the ducky birds?"
But the baby started to…

scream!

So his brother said,
"If you let me hold the bag,
I'll let you hold my ice-cream."

Then the boy said,
"Quiet all you quack-quacks!
And stop pushing,
you're all going to get fed."
And he put his hand in the paper bag
and brought out a handful of bread.

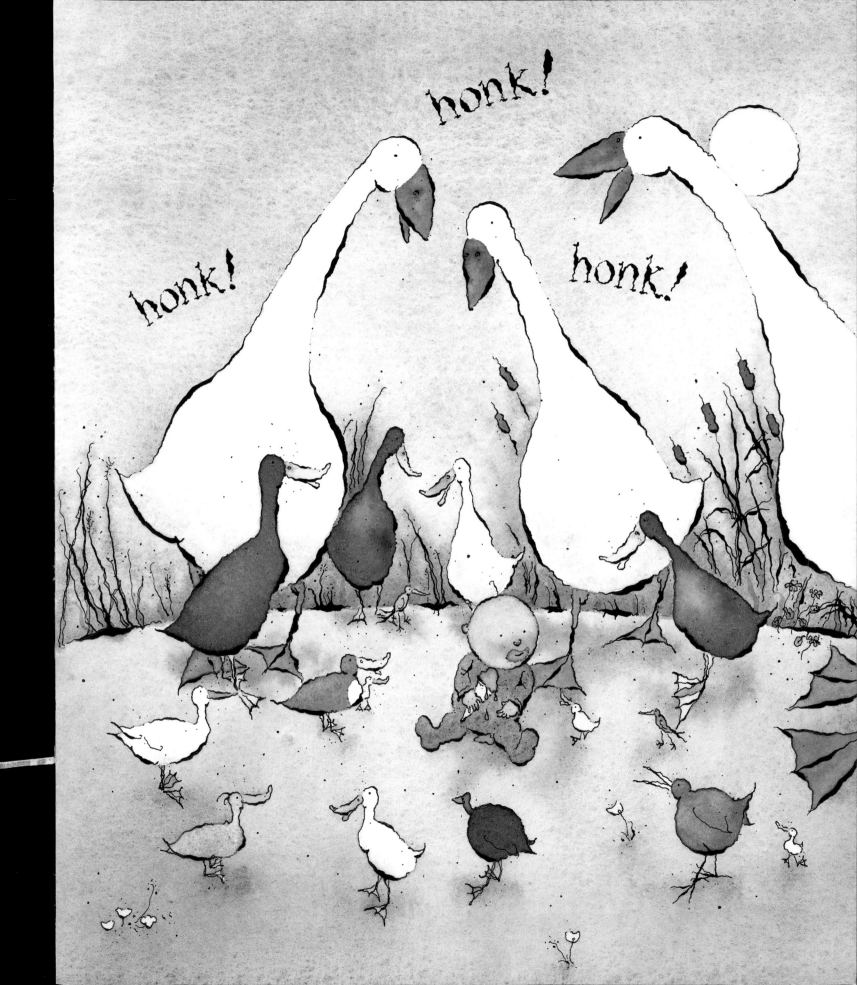

So all the birds went quiet…

and the band stopped playing too…

And all the animals stopped making a noise,
including the animals in the zoo.

And suddenly the baby realized
they were all waiting for a crumb!
So he gave the ice-cream back
and he took a great big handful
of bread and…

threw!

all the ducky birds some.

Then all the hungry ducky birds
were ever so glad they'd come,
And instead of going...

honk! honk!
quacky quack-
quack!

all the birdies said...